This edition published by Parragon Books Ltd in 2015

Parragon Books Ltd
Chartist House
15–17 Trim Street
Bath BA1 1HA, UK
www.parragon.com

Based on the episode written by Ashley Mendoza
Adapted by Bill Scollon
Illustrated by Loter, Inc.

ISBN 978-1-4723-9655-6

Printed in China

MICKEY MOUSE CLUBHOUSE

A Goofy Fairy Tale

PaRragon

Bath • New York • Cologne • Melbourne • Delhi
Hong Kong • Shenzhen • Singapore • Amsterdam

Tonight is story night and Mickey is going to read a bedtime story from the Clubhouse library.

"How will we decide which story to read?" Minnie wonders.

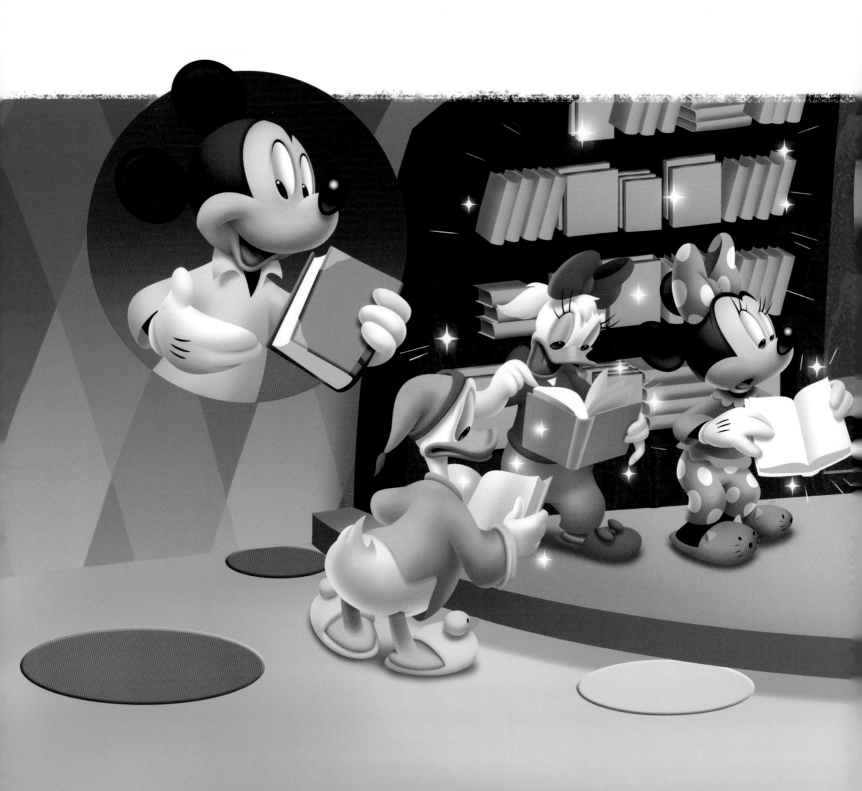

"I'll use magic to pick a book," says Goofy. "Book-a-doodle-doo. Fly away and shoo!"

Oh, no! Goofy uses the wrong magic words. All the stories disappear! "Golly," he says. "I goofed up."

Mickey goes to Professor Von Drake to ask for help.
"Professor, where have our stories gone?"
The professor uses a remote control to open a magic door.

"Your stories can be found in a gold book with a heart,
a diamond and a rose on its cover," the professor says.
"The book is in the beast's castle in the Land of Fairy Tales."

Suddenly, Goofy slips and
falls through the magic door.
   "My remote control is broken!"
cries the professor. "Goofy's
stuck in the Land of Fairy Tales!"

   "Goofy can't get the gold storybook all
by himself," says Daisy.
   "You can do it, pal!" Mickey calls to Goofy.

In the Land of Fairy Tales, Goofy finds himself dressed in new, fairy-tale clothes. Before long, Goofy is lost.

"Gawrsh," says Goofy. "Which way leads to the beast's castle?"
"Go right!" answers a tiny voice.

Goofy is so surprised he slips
and falls to the ground!
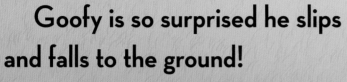
"You're a goofy fella!" says a small knight.
"Goofyfella!" laughs Goofy. "That can
be my fairy-tale name."

"We're Chip and Dale Thumb," says Chip,
the small knight.
"But we've got to go," adds Dale Thumb.
"Big problem at the castle!"

Soon, Goofyfella meets Pied Piper Donald and Pluto the Merry Dog. They're trying to lead ducklings to a pond.

Goofyfella wants to teach Pied Piper Donald a new song, but he drops the flute and breaks it! "Oh, Toodles!" he says.

Toodles's cousin, Goofles, arrives with four
Mouseketools: suction cups, sticky tape, an oar
and one Mystery Mouseketool.
Goofyfella uses the tape to fix the flute.

When Pied Piper Donald plays the new song,
the ducklings line up and follow him!

Goofyfella soon finds himself lost deep in the woods.
He runs into Hansel and Gretel Mouse. They're lost, too!

"Maybe somebody in that house can help us,"
says Goofyfella.
"Hello!" a voice calls from the house.
It's Witch Clarabelle!

Witch Clarabelle is making a big batch of Merry Muffins,
but she can't find her mixing spoon.

"I can help!" says Goofyfella.

He calls for Goofles and chooses the oar Mouseketool.

Goofyfella accidentally knocks a basket of berries
into the batter!
"Ah, that's just what it needs," says Witch Clarabelle.
"Can you help me get to the castle?" says Goofyfella.

"Just follow the diamond shapes,"
says Witch Clarabelle.
Goofyfella says goodbye to his
new friends and hurries on his way.

The diamond shapes lead Goofyfella to a crystal mountain
and the beast's castle is at the top!

Goofyfella starts to climb the mountain, but the path is
too slippery and he slides straight back down!

Goofyfella calls Goofles who has two Mouseketools left: the suction cups and the Mystery Mouseketool. He chooses the suction cups! He puts them on his shoes and marches right up the mountain.

Goofyfella sees Chip and Dale Thumb at the castle door.

"We've come to rescue Daisy Beauty," Dale Thumb tells him.

"But we're so small," says Chip Thumb, "the beast can't hear us knocking."

"I'll just ring this bell," Goofyfella says.

But he pulls on the rope too hard, the bell falls on his head!

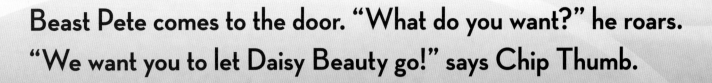

Beast Pete comes to the door. "What do you want?" he roars.
"We want you to let Daisy Beauty go!" says Chip Thumb.

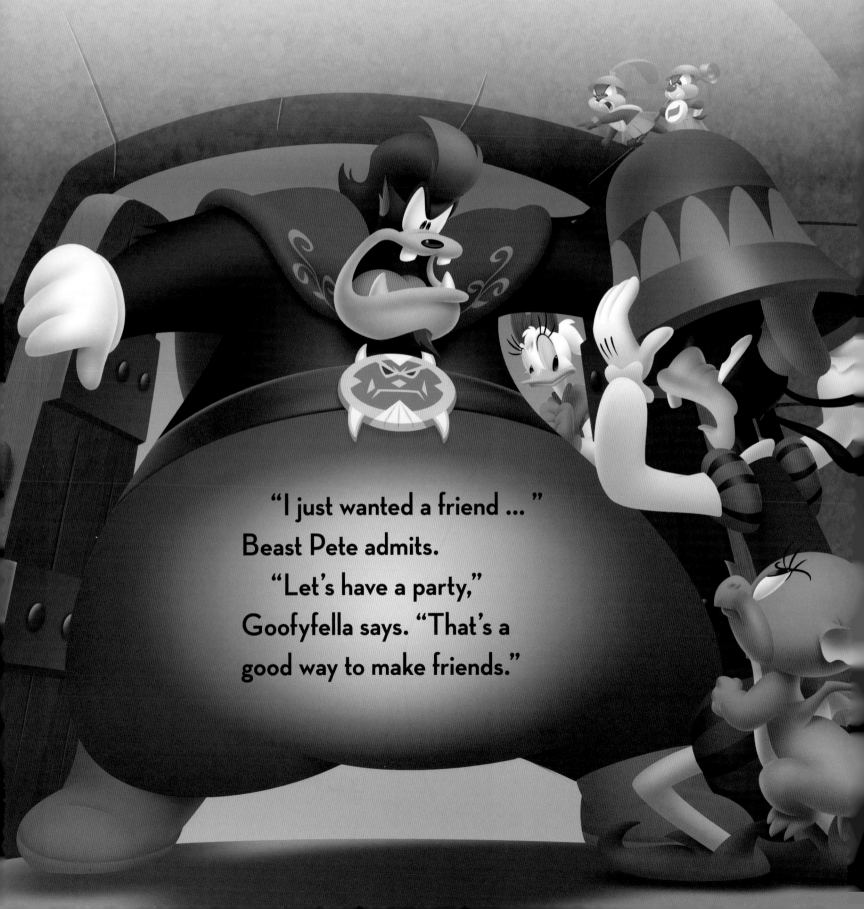

"I just wanted a friend ..."
Beast Pete admits.
"Let's have a party,"
Goofyfella says. "That's a
good way to make friends."

"Great idea!" says Beast Pete.
He turns to Daisy Beauty.
"Will you be my guest?" he asks her politely.
Daisy Beauty realizes Beast Pete is really very kind.

"Yes," she answers. "We can be friends, too."
Suddenly, Beast Pete turns into a prince.
Daisy Beauty's friendship broke the spell!

"I owe this all to you, Goofyfella," Prince Pete says.
"How can I repay you?"

"Well, I'm looking for the gold storybook," Goofyfella says.

"If the book is in my library," says Prince Pete, "it's yours."

Prince Pete's library is stacked high with books.

"What does the gold storybook look like?" he asks.

"It's decorated with three shapes," says Goofyfella. "A heart, a diamond and a rose."

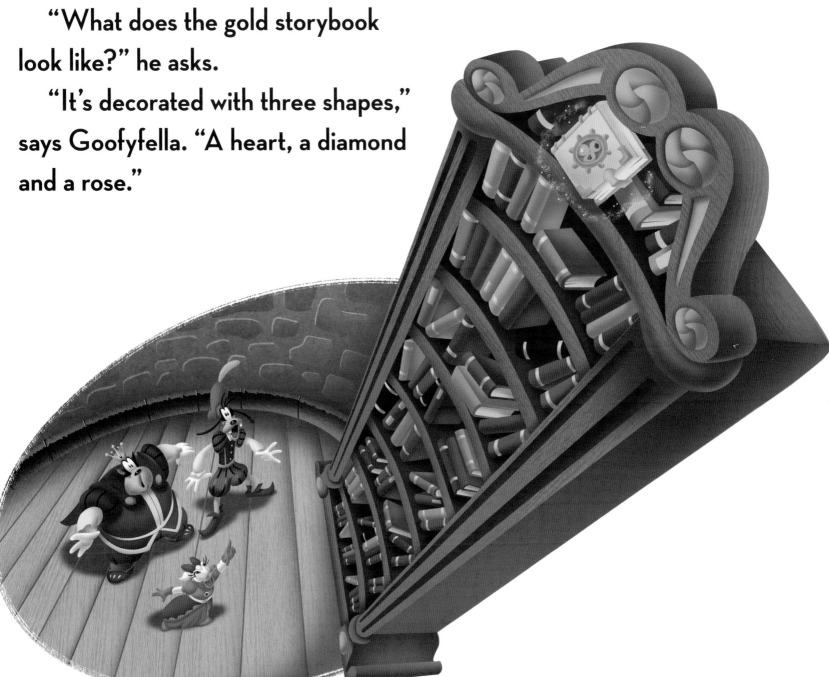

"I see it!" shouts Daisy Beauty. "But it's up so high."

"I know just what to do," says Goofyfella. "Oh, Goofles!"

The Mystery Mouseketool
is a bunch of balloons!
Goofyfella holds on to them
and floats to the top shelf!
He grabs the gold storybook.

"I've got it!" shouts Goofyfella.
"But how will I get down?"
Chip and Dale Thumb come to the
rescue, popping the balloons one at a time.
Goofyfella floats safely back to the ground.

It's time for Goofyfella to go home.

Prince Pete asks Rosalie the dragon to give Goofyfella a ride. Goofyfella holds the gold storybook tight and waves goodbye to his new fairy-tale friends.

At the Clubhouse, the professor finally gets the remote control working. He presses the button and opens the door. Rosalie the dragon flies to the magic door and Goofy steps right through.

"Goofy!" yells Mickey. "You did it!"
"I sure did," says Goofy. "Just in time for a bedtime story!"

Mickey opens the gold storybook and the
missing stories fly back into their books!
    "So, what story should we read?" says Goofy.
    "We want to hear your story!" Daisy says.
"How'd you find the book?"

    "Well," begins Goofy, "I guess you
could say I found it in my own goofy way!"

The End